To:

From:

Written by Louise Gikow
Illustrated by Tom Leigh

BY CONTEMPO®

ISBN: 0-307-70353-3

SOMEONE LIKE YOU

A Muppet™ Pick-Me-Up Book

Someone like you is very rare,
A special friend beyond compare.

Someone like you is lots of fun
And makes me feel I'm number one.

Someone like you is never cross
And always lets me be the boss.

Someone like you is helpful, too,
And makes things right when I feel blue.

Someone like you just seems to know
Exactly where I'd like to go.

Someone like you is always there
To pick me up with love and care.

Someone like you is kind and sweet,
The nicest person I could meet.

Someone like you is someone who
Is always faithful, through and through.

Someone like you is hard to find.
You never leave me in a bind.

That's why I can't believe it's true,
That I have found. . .

Someone like you!